FOR ELLIE
(MY FELLOW FOOD FIEND)
x

First published 2017 by Two Hoots
This edition published 2018 by Two Hoots
an imprint of Pan Macmillan
20 New Wharf Road, London N1 9RR
Associated companies throughout the world
www.panmacmillan.com
ISBN 978-1-5098-3462-4
Text and illustrations copyright © Morag Hood 2017
Moral rights asserted.

1 3 5 7 9 8 6 4 2
A CIP catalogue record for this book is available from the British Library.
Printed in China
The illustrations in this book were created using lino print and collage.

www.twohootsbooks.com

MORAG HOOD

I AM BAT

TW🦉 HOOTS

I AM BAT.

I do not
like mornings.

I like **CHERRIES.**

They are my

FAVOURITE

of all things.

They are JUICY and RED and DELICIOUS and . . .

...THEY ARE MINE.

Do **NOT**

take my cherries.

If you take my

cherries

I will be

ANGRY.

I will be **FEROCIOUS** like a lion.

(But smaller and with wings.)

I WILL KNOW IF
YOU TAKE ONE.

My
CHERRIES!
Some of them are
MISSING.

Where did
they go?

Who stole my

CHERRIES?

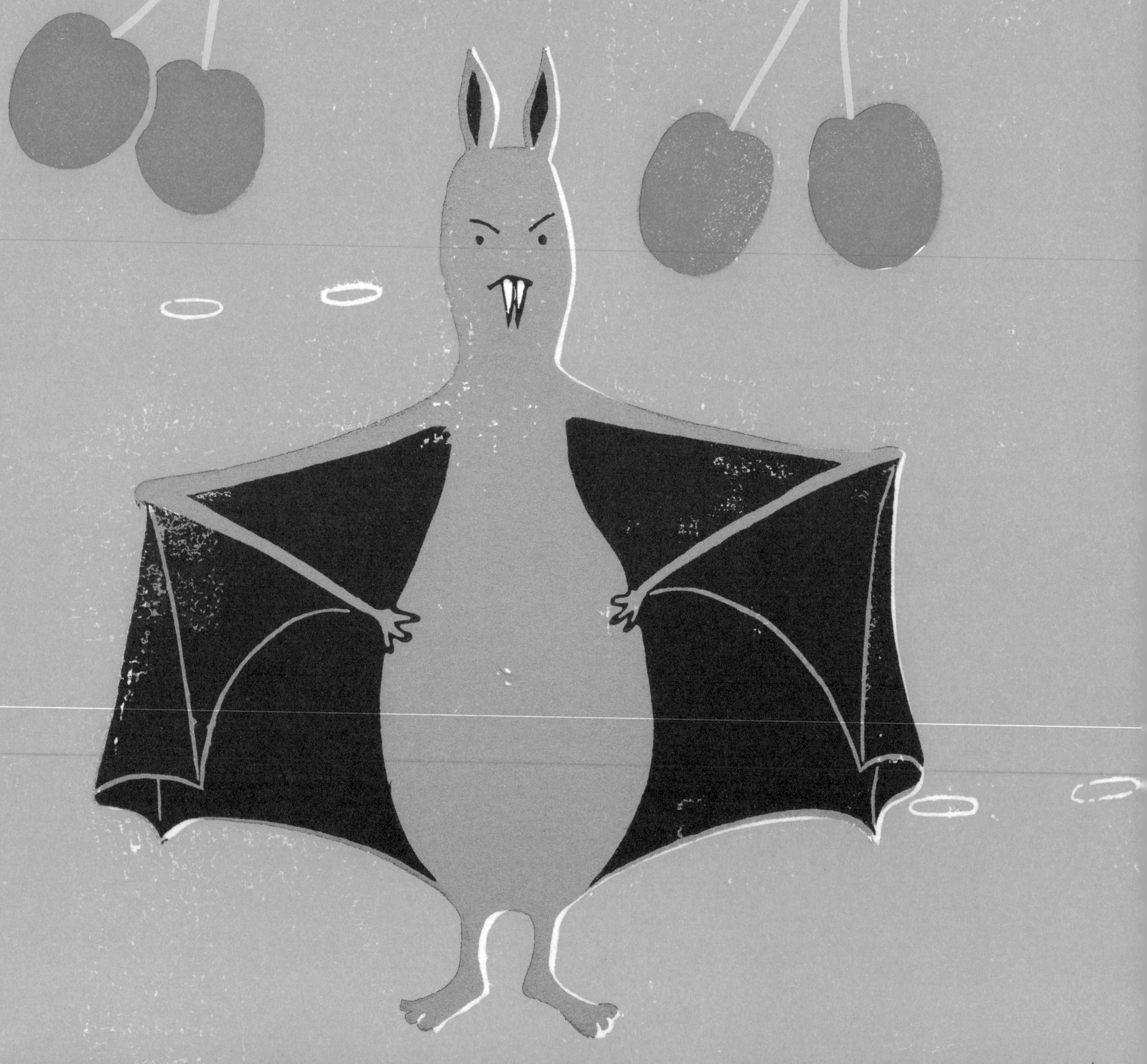

Was it

YOU?

I will **NEVER** be happy again.

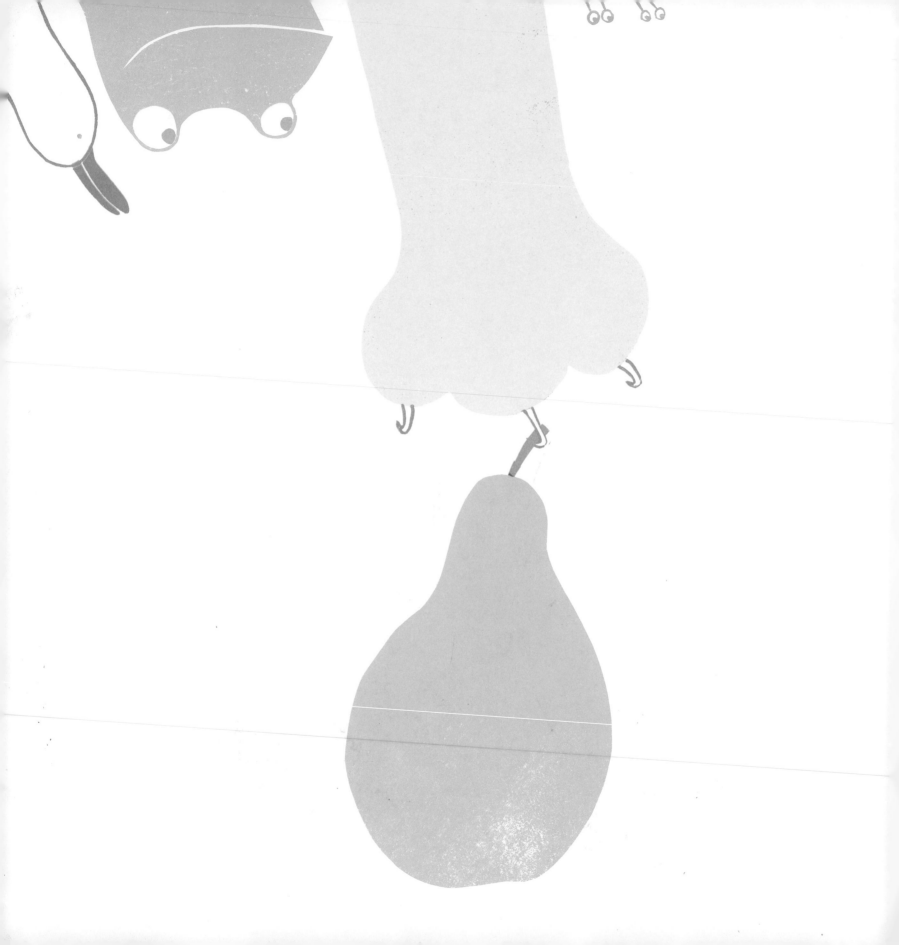

Ooh . . .

A PEAR!

I like **PEARS.**

I AM BAT.

DO NOT TAKE MY PEAR.

Bat's recipe for

JUICY RED DELICIOUS CHERRIES

Ingredients

Cherries

Method

Take one cherry and add another cherry.

Mix.

Taste.

Add a lot more cherries.

Check for lions.

Serve.

Serves one.